IMAGINE THAT

Licensed exclusively to Imagine That Publishing Ltd
Tide Mill Way, Woodbridge, Suffolk, IP12 1AP, UK
www.imaginethat.com
Copyright © 2020 Imagine That Group Ltd
All rights reserved
2 4 6 8 9 7 5 3 1
Manufactured in China

Written by Susie Linn
Illustrated by Dubravka Kolanovic

ISBN 978-1-78700-910-3

A catalogue record for this book is available from the British Library

‘For J & J.’ SL

I need a hug!

Written by

Susie Linn

Illustrated by

Dubravka Kolanovic

As the early morning sun rose over the zoo,
the animals were waking up. All except for
Boo the bushbaby. Like all bushbabies,
Boo slept in the daytime, so he was
ready for bed.

But where was Mummy?
Boo couldn't sleep without
his mummy's special bedtime hug.

Boo looked everywhere, but Mummy
was nowhere to be seen.

So Boo went to see Lion.

'I need a hug!'
Boo said to Lion.

Very gently, Lion lifted
Boo in one big paw and ...

... hugged him close.

'Thank you, Lion,' spluttered Boo, with a mouthful of Lion's mane, 'but your hug is too **hairy!**'

So Boo went to see Giraffe.

'I need a hug!'

Boo called up to Giraffe.

Giraffe stopped what she was doing, wrapped her long neck around Boo and ...

... hugged and lifted
him all at once!

'Thank you, Giraffe,'
gulped Boo, looking down
at the ground below,
'but your hug is
too **high!**'

So Boo went to see Penguin.

'I need a hug!'
Boo called to Penguin.

Penguin looked up from his breakfast,
stretched out his flippers and ...

... pulled Boo towards him.

'Thank you, Penguin,' choked Boo, holding his nose,
'but your hug is too **fishy!**'

So Boo went to see Kangaroo.

'I need a hug!'
Boo shouted to Kangaroo,
as she bounded past.

Without stopping, Kangaroo swept Boo off his feet and ...

... hugged him as she
hopped on her way.

'Thank you, Kangaroo,'
Boo managed to say,
in between each huge jump,
'but your hug is much too **bouncy!**'

Boo was tired and he needed a
bedtime hug more than ever.
Perhaps Macaw could help.

'I need a hug!'
yelled Boo above Macaw's
loud squawks.

SQUAWK!

Macaw carried on squawking,
spread his wings and ...

... hugged Boo to his feathery chest.

'Thank you, Macaw!' yelled Boo,
'but your hug is just too **noisy!**'

SQUAWK!

'What about Polar Bear?'
wondered Boo.

'I need a hug!'
said Boo, looking up
into Polar Bear's
friendly face.

Ever so carefully, Polar Bear opened her arms and ...

... gathered Boo up into her soft, white fur.

'Thank you, Polar Bear,' yawned Boo, squinting, 'but your hug is too **bright!**'

What was Boo to do?
It was time for bed – and still there was no
Mummy, and still no just-right bedtime hug.

'Too **wrinkly!**'

'Too **bumpy!**'

'Too **tight!**'

'Too **tickly!**'

'Too **big!**'

'Too **wet!**'

'I don't need a hug that's too **hairy** ...

too **high** ...

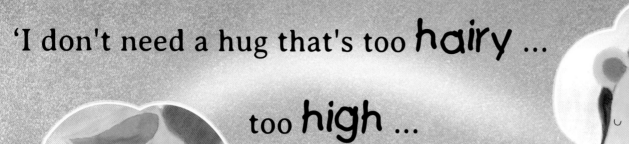

too **fishy** ...

too **bouncy** ...

too **noisy** ...

too **bright** ...

too **wrinkly** ...

too **bumpy** ...

too **tight** ...

too **tickly** ...

too **big** ...

or too **wet**,' whispered Boo to himself.

'I need a hug that's ... that's ...'

Just then, Boo felt warm, familiar,
comfy arms around him.

'... that's just right!'
he shouted in delight.

'Sleep tight, Boo,' said Mummy, as she gave him
the cuddliest, snuggliest, just-right bedtime
hug in all the world.

The End